Pig Has a Plan

by **Ethan Long**

I Like to Read®

HOLIDAY HOUSE • NEW YORK

Pig wants to nap.

Hen wants to saw.

Cow wants to gab.

Cat wants to pop.

Dog wants to tap.

Rat wants to mix.

Hog wants to hum.

Pup wants to bop.

Fly wants to sip.

Pig cannot nap.

Pig has a plan.

SIP
SIP SIP

Now Pig can nap.

I Like to Read® books, created by award-winning
picture book artists as well as talented newcomers,
instill confidence and the joy of reading in new readers.

We want to hear every new reader say, "I like to read!"

Visit our website for flash cards, activities, and more about the series:
www.holidayhouse.com/I-Like-to-Read/
#ILTR
This book has been tested by an educational expert
and determined to be a guided reading level B.

To Azalia and Amir.
Love, Uncle Stinky

I LIKE TO READ® is a registered trademark of Holiday House Publishing, Inc.

Copyright © 2012 by Ethan Long
All Rights Reserved
HOLIDAY HOUSE is registered in the U.S. Patent and Trademark Office.
Printed and bound in September 2020 at Toppan Leefung, DongGuan City, China.
The artwork was created with black Prismacolor colored pencils
on bristol board and colored digitally on a Mac.
www.holidayhouse.com
5 7 9 10 8 6 4

Library of Congress Cataloging-in-Publication Data
Long, Ethan.
Pig has a plan / by Ethan Long. — 1st ed.
p. cm. — (I like to read)
Summary: Pig is trying to take a nap, but his friends
are making all kinds of noise.
ISBN 978-0-8234-2428-3 (hardcover)
[1. Naps (Sleep)—Fiction. 2. Noise—Fiction. 3. Pigs—Fiction.
4. Domestic animals—Fiction.] I. Title.
PZ7.L8453Pi 2012
[E]—dc23
2011041294

ISBN 978-0-8234-3880-8 (paperback)

I Like to Read®

Visit http://www.holidayhouse.com/I-Like-to-Read/ for more about I Like to Read®
books, including flash cards, reproducibles, and the complete list of titles.